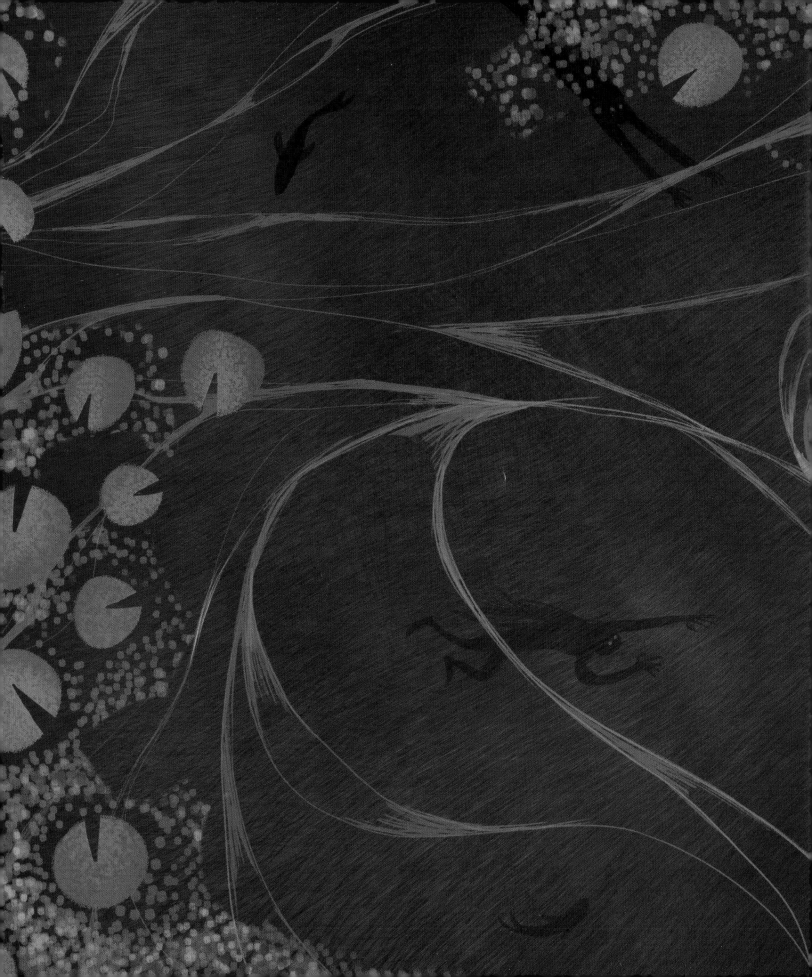

THE SONG THAT CALLED THEM HOME

DAVID A. ROBERTSON

ILLUSTRATED BY
MAYA McKIBBIN

tundra

On a clear day in the middle of summer, Lauren and her little brother, James, went on a trip to the land with their moshom.

It was a long journey, and when they arrived,
Moshom fell asleep.

While Moshom dreamed his dreams, Lauren's
stomach began to rumble. She imagined a big fish
they could all share and took James into the canoe
to catch their supper.

But Lauren hadn't paddled a canoe herself before,
so they drifted farther and farther from the shore.

In the middle of the lake, James' fishing hook dove underneath the surface, while Lauren stirred the water to attract fish.

Around them, tiny circles got
bigger and bigger.

Suddenly, the circles rolled into waves that crashed against the canoe, rocking it back and forth, back and forth, back and forth.

The children tumbled overboard,
and the swirling water pulled them in.

Lauren looked around for James, but
didn't see him until he cried out.

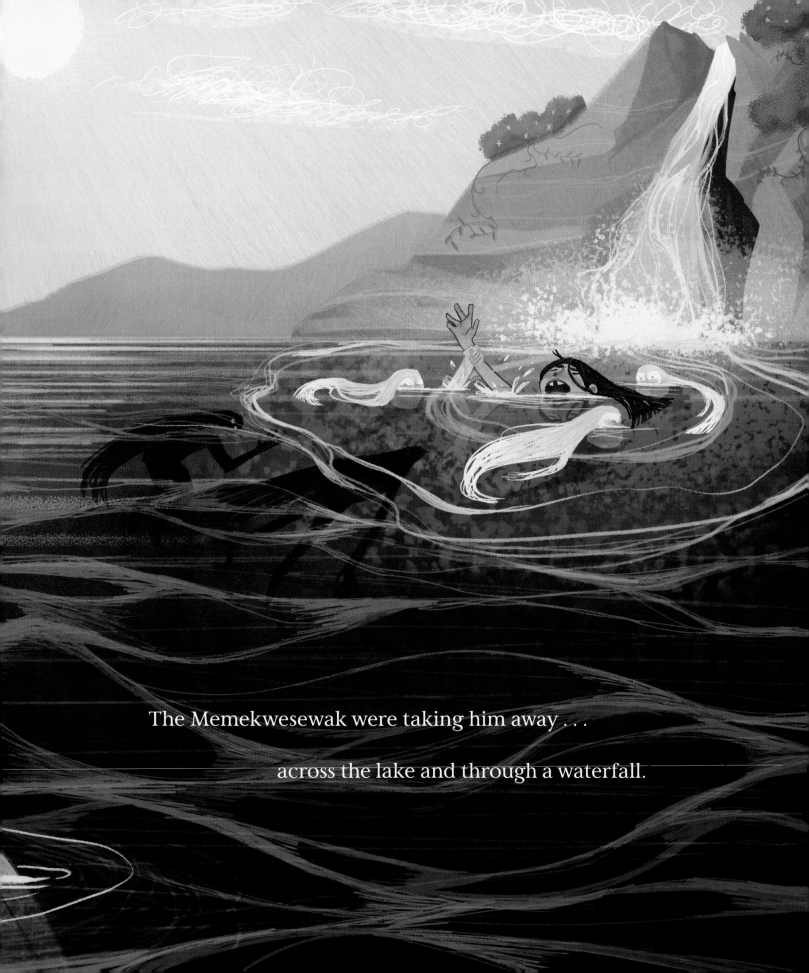

The Memekwesewak were taking him away . . .

across the lake and through a waterfall.

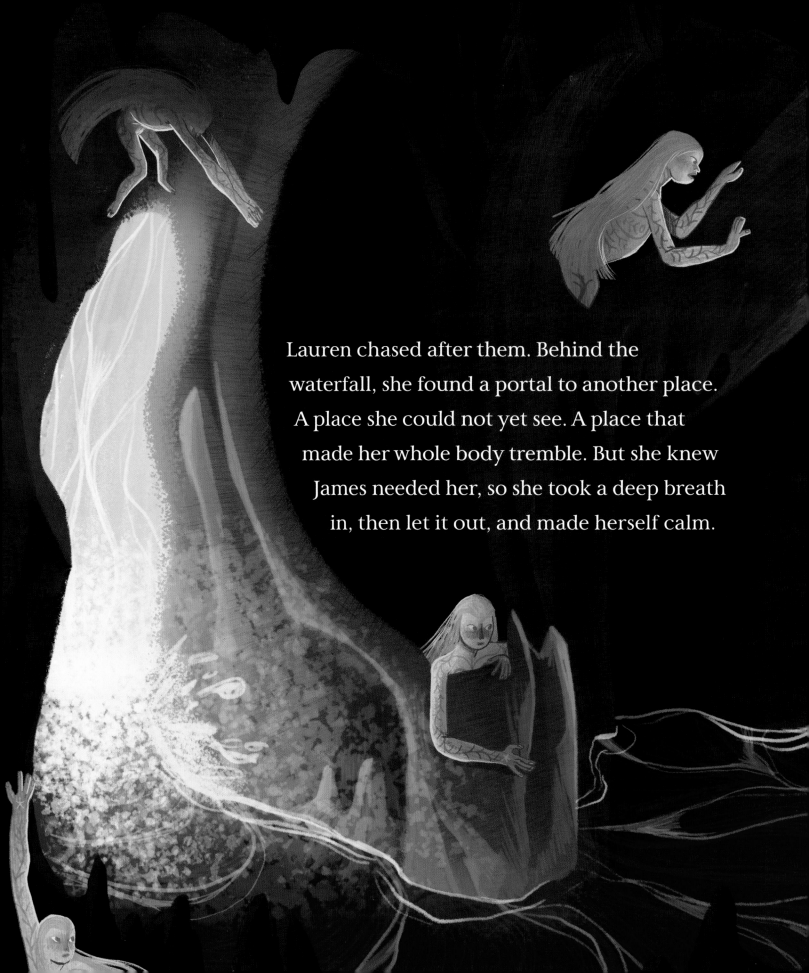

Lauren chased after them. Behind the
waterfall, she found a portal to another place.
A place she could not yet see. A place that
made her whole body tremble. But she knew
James needed her, so she took a deep breath
in, then let it out, and made herself calm.

She squeezed between
rocks, swam down a long,
dark tunnel, and went where
the water went . . .

right into the other side.

Lauren followed the bends and curves of the watery pathway, searching for James.

She swam past thick green forests under vast blue skies.

Then she came to an island, where she saw figures moving in a round dance and a fire with flames reaching to the stars.

And there was James dancing his best, joined together with all the rest.

Lauren tried to pull him away but instead found herself linking hands with the Memekwesewak.

She began to move with the others, right beside her little brother.

They shuffled their feet, swung their arms
and danced along to the Memekwesewak's song.

Way-oh, hey
Way-oh, hey
Way-oh, hey, hey, hey

What a bright, beautiful
summer day,
way-hey, way-hey!
We don't want you
to ever go,
way-oh, way-oh!
We want you
to always stay,
way-hey, way-hey!
What a beautiful place
to call your home,
way-oh, way-oh!

Way-oh, hey
Way-oh, hey
Way-oh, hey, hey, hey

They danced faster and faster for minutes that turned into hours that turned into days. They danced so long that Lauren forgot why she had come at all.

But then they heard another song that sounded like distant thunder.

THUM
THUMP

THUM
THUMP

THUM
THUMP

Lauren stopped dancing to listen, and so too
did James. The children could feel the drum in
their chests, just like the beat of their hearts.

The Memekwesewak let go of their hands
and plunged into the water from the land.

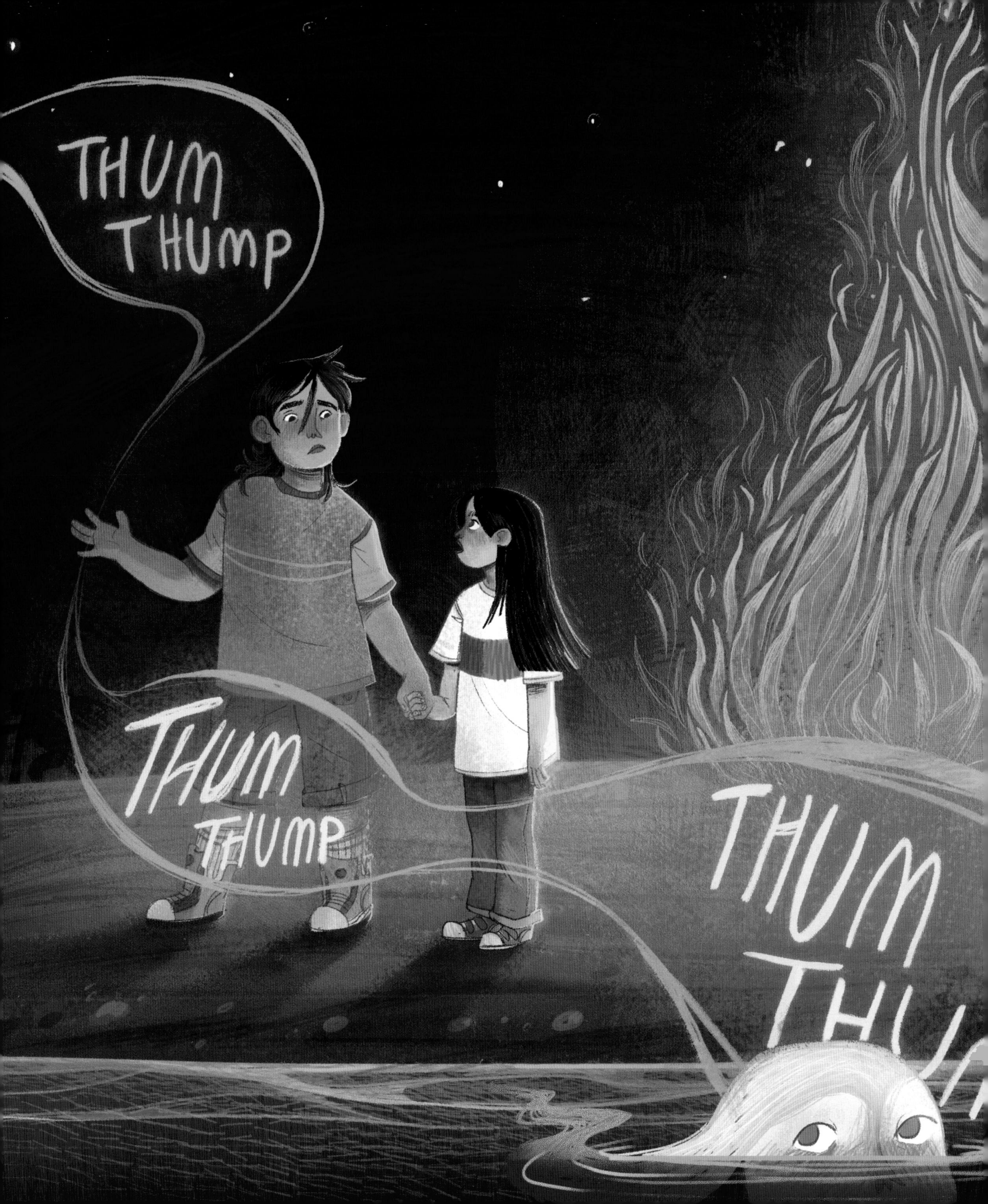
THUM THUMP
THUM THUMP
THUM THU

Lauren and James danced once more,
toward the song, moving their feet
to its familiar rhythm.

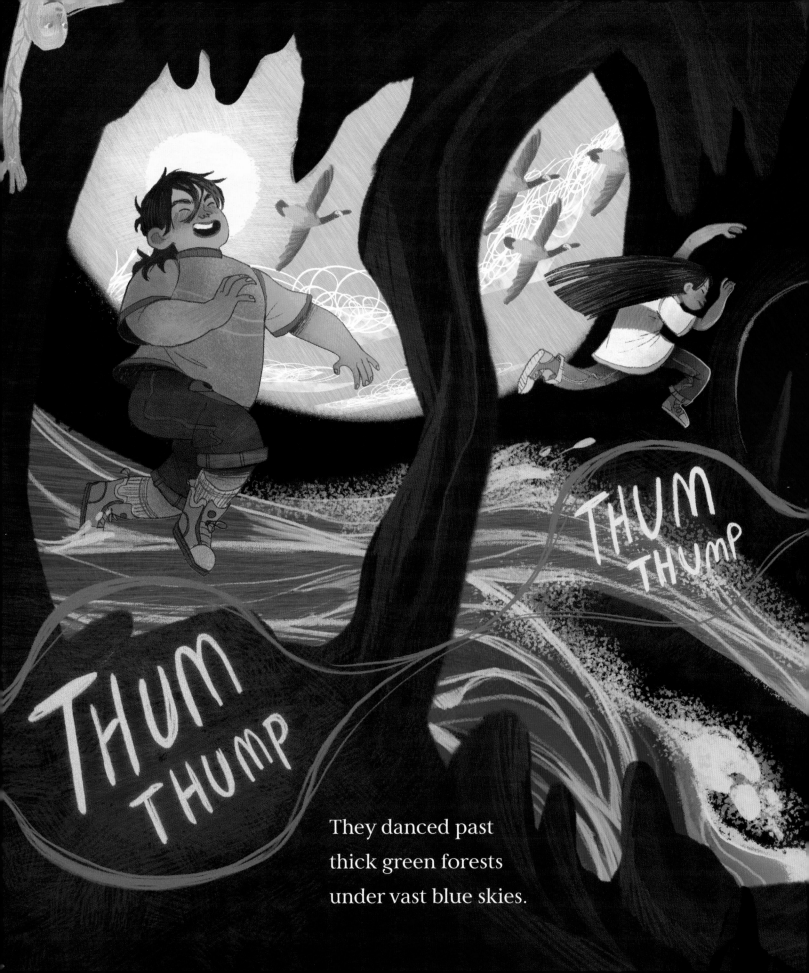

They danced past
thick green forests
under vast blue skies.

Up they climbed, toward the portal, then in.

They squeezed between rocks,
swam down a long, dark tunnel,
and went where the water went . . .

right into the
other side.

THUM
THUMP

THUM
THUMP

Lauren and James swam to Moshom, who was waiting
at the shore, singing and playing his drum, hoping
that his grandchildren would one day come.

That night, they danced around a fire
to the song that had called them home.

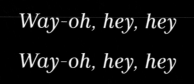

Way-oh, hey, hey

Way-oh, hey, hey

Come back! The sun is falling!

The soft white light will help you see!

Come back! The moon is calling!

How beautiful the night can be!

Way-oh, hey, hey

Way-oh, hey, hey

Come back! You've been gone so long!

What places have you found to roam!

Come back! Hear my welcome song!

My beating drum will guide you home!

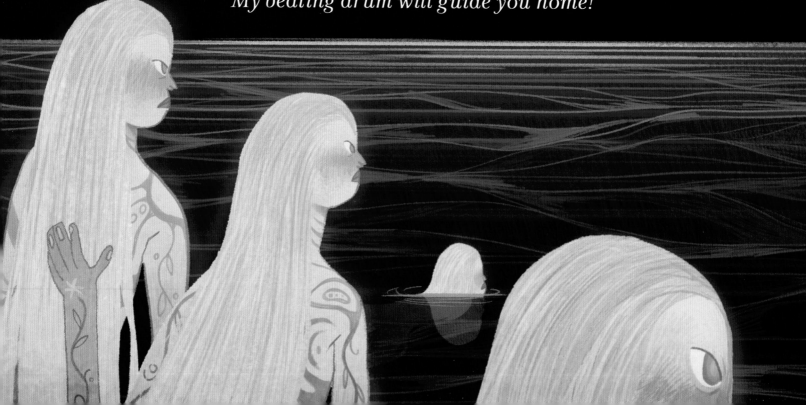

AUTHOR'S NOTE
ABOUT THE MEMEKWESEWAK

Indigenous communities across Turtle Island have stories of the Memekwesewak (Meh-meh-gwee-see-wack), or little people. They are one of two humanoid races on Mother Earth, the other being humans like you and me. Memekwesewak live between rocks, in the rapids, amid the trees of the land that provides us with life. They are mischievous. It is said that one of their favorite things to do is to crawl out of the rocks and capsize canoes. Children are far more likely to see them. Memekwesewak have a soft spot for children and will help when they are in trouble or sad.

One day, when my father was a boy living on the trapline, he saw a small canoe occupied by Memekwesewak. The canoe moved across the water, toward a waterfall. It didn't stop. It went through the waterfall and then suddenly disappeared.

I've heard stories of Elders who leave miniature clothing out on their porch at night for the Memekwesewak and in the morning discover the clothing is gone. If you're ever out on the land, keep your eyes open, because you may just see the Memekwesewak.

For the kids. Never stop dancing, and watch for our little friends. — **DAR**

Thanks to the friends and family who have helped me have homes
as I figured out where to be during these turbulently shifting times. — **MM**

Tundra Books, an imprint of Tundra Book Group,
a division of Penguin Random House of Canada Limited

Library and Archives Canada Cataloguing in Publication

Title: The song that called them home / David A. Robertson ; illustrated by Maya McKibbin.
Names: Robertson, David, 1977- author. | McKibbin, Maya, 1995- illustrator.
Identifiers: Canadiana (print) 20210152095 | Canadiana (ebook) 20210152109 |
ISBN 9780735266704 (hardcover) | ISBN 9780735266711 (EPUB)
Classification: LCC PS8585.O32115 S66 2022 | DDC jC813/.6—dc23

Published simultaneously in the United States of America by Tundra Books of Northern New York,
an imprint of Tundra Book Group, a division of Penguin Random House of Canada Limited

Library of Congress Control Number: 2021949377

Acquired by Tara Walker
Edited by Elizabeth Kribs
Designed by John Martz
The artwork in this book was drawn digitally.
The text was set in Carrig.

Printed in China

www.penguinrandomhouse.ca

1   2   3   4   5   27   26   25   24   23

Penguin
Random House
tundra   TUNDRA BOOKS